The
Tiara
Club

✦ AT RUBY MANSIONS ✦

The Tiara Club

Princess Charlotte *and the* Birthday Ball

Princess Katie *and the* Silver Pony

Princess Daisy *and the* Dazzling Dragon

Princess Alice *and the* Magical Mirror

Princess Sophia *and the* Sparkling Surprise

Princess Emily *and the* Substitute Fairy

———◦◎◦———

The Tiara Club at Silver Towers

Princess Charlotte *and the* Enchanted Rose

Princess Katie *and the* Mixed-up Potion

Princess Daisy *and the* Magical Merry-Go-Round

Princess Alice *and the* Glass Slipper

Princess Sophia *and the* Prince's Party

Princess Emily *and the* Wishing Star

———◦◎◦———

The Tiara Club at Ruby Mansions

Princess Chloe *and the* Primrose Petticoats

Princess Jessica *and the* Best-Friend Bracelet

Princess Olivia *and the* Velvet Cape

Princess Lauren *and the* Diamond Necklace

Princess Amy *and the* Forgetting Dust

~ VIVIAN FRENCH ~

The Tiara Club

✦ AT RUBY MANSIONS ✦

Princess Georgia
~ AND THE ~
Shimmering Pearl

KATHERINE TEGEN BOOKS
HarperTrophy®
An Imprint of HarperCollinsPublishers

The Tiara Club at Ruby Mansions:
Princess Georgia and the Shimmering Pearl
Text copyright © 2008 by Vivian French
Illustrations copyright © 2008 by Orchard Books
www.harpercollinschildrens.com

Library of Congress Catalog Card Number: 2007905257
ISBN 978-0-06-143486-0

Typography by Amy Ryan
❖
First U.S. edition, 2008

For the truly delightful Princess Anna,
daughter of the wonderful Queen Janet
—V. F.

The Royal Palace Academy
for the Preparation of Perfect Princesses
(Known to our students as "The Princess Academy")

OUR SCHOOL MOTTO:
A Perfect Princess always thinks of others before herself,
and is kind, caring, and truthful.

Ruby Mansions offers a complete education for Tiara Club princesses with emphasis on the creative arts. The curriculum includes:

Innovative Ideas for our Friendship Festival

Designing Floral Bouquets (all thorns will be removed)

Ballet for Grace and Poise

A visit to the Diamond Exhibition
(on the joyous occasion of Queen Fabiola's birthday)

Our principal, Queen Fabiola, is present at all times, and students are in the excellent care of the head fairy godmother, Fairy G., and her assistant, Fairy Angora.

OUR RESIDENT STAFF & VISITING EXPERTS INCLUDE:

KING BERNARDO IV *(Ruby Mansions Governor)*

LADY ARAMINTA *(Princess Academy Matron)*

LADY HARRIS *(Secretary to Queen Fabiola)*

QUEEN MOTHER MATILDA *(Etiquette, Posture, and Flower Arranging)*

We award tiara points to encourage our
Tiara Club princesses toward the next level.
All princesses who earn enough points at Ruby
Mansions will attend a celebration ball, where they
will be presented with their Ruby Sashes.

Ruby Sash Tiara Club princesses are invited
to go on to Pearl Palace, our very special
residence for Perfect Princesses, where they may
continue their education at a higher level.

PLEASE NOTE:

Princesses are expected to arrive
at the Academy with a *minimum* of:

TWENTY BALL GOWNS
*(with all necessary hoops,
petticoats, etc.)*

TWELVE DAY-DRESSES

SEVEN GOWNS
*suitable for garden parties
and other special daytime
occasions*

TWELVE TIARAS

DANCING SHOES
five pairs

VELVET SLIPPERS
three pairs

RIDING BOOTS
two pairs

*Cloaks, muffs, stoles, gloves,
and other essential
accessories, as required*

Hello! I'm very pleased to meet you. I'm Princess Georgia. And Chloe, Jessica, Olivia, Lauren, and Amy share the Poppy Room with me—and we're very best friends. We're trying to be Perfect Princesses. But—guess what?

It isn't always easy.

I'm so glad you're here at Ruby Mansions with us—but watch out for the horrible twins, Diamonde and Gruella.

They're so mean.

But we'll take care of you.

You're our friend!

Chapter One

$\mathcal{P}$rincess Chloe started sneezing first. She sneezed twice over break-fast and about fifty times during our first class, which was Velvet Trains and How to Wear Them. And by lunchtime, she just couldn't stop. And her nose kept running and her eyes were red and she looked terrible. Poor Chloe!

"I thig I'd better tell Fairy G. that I'b dot feeling very well," she said.

Of course Fairy G. took Chloe straight to Ruby Pillows, which is

where we go when we're sick. It's a lovely airy room up at the top of Ruby Mansions, and we don't mind being there at all, even though Lady Araminta is very strict. She's the nurse in charge of Ruby Pillows. Fairy G. (our school

Fairy Godmother) comes to visit a lot, too, and to check that everything's all right. It's weird—you'd think a Fairy Godmother would just wave her wand and make everyone better, but she won't. She says it's cheating and a waste of good magic.

By the middle of the afternoon, Princess Lauren was sneezing as well, and that night there were only four of us princesses in the Poppy Room: Amy, Jessica, Olivia, and me. The others were tucked in at Ruby Pillows, sniffing and snuffling and feeling miserable.

"Do you think I might catch it

next?" Jessica asked hopefully as she climbed into bed. "There's that test tomorrow, and I just know I'm going to fail. I'll never be able to Design a Floral Bouquet to Present to a Very Special Princess, but if I catch the bug, I'll miss the exam!"

Olivia giggled. "'Now, princesses,

please remember that a Perfect Princess *never* makes a mistake, and *always* knows how to spell Variegated Nasturtiums!'"

Olivia is so funny—she sounded exactly like Queen Mother Matilda! We all laughed, but my laugh turned into a sneeze.

"Oops!" I said, and fished under

my pillow for a hankie. "Maybe it'll be me that misses the test."

Jessica made a face at me. "That's not fair. You're sure to pass—you're great at flower arranging."

"You're the best of all of us," Amy told me and she giggled. "It makes the twins so jealous!"

Olivia nodded. "Princess Diamonde went absolutely purple after it was your turn to do the flowers for assembly, and I'm sure Princess Gruella tried to knock the vases over."

"She did," I said. *"Atchoo! ATCHOOOO!"*

Amy looked at me anxiously. "Do you feel sick? Do you want me to get Fairy G.?"

I shook my head. "I'll be okay for tonight," I said, although I was beginning to feel a bit woozy.

But by the morning, I felt terrible and I didn't even manage to wish the others good luck before Fairy G. whisked me away to Ruby Pillows.

But none of us took part in the exam. When I woke up later on that morning and looked around, I saw every bed was full. All six of us from the Poppy Room were there,

and the twins, Diamonde and
Gruella, were too.

"I feel terrible!" Diamonde
wailed.

"You're not as bad as I am," Gruella told her. "I feel awful!"

"That's why you're here," Lady Araminta said crisply, and she tucked in Diamonde's and Gruella's covers so tightly they could hardly breathe.

Chapter Two

*F*or the first couple of days, we all felt too sick to talk very much. On the third day, I woke up feeling a lot better. Lady Araminta came to take my temperature.

"Excellent. We'll keep you here for a day or two more, just in case, but you're doing very nicely. Now, you can get out of bed if you feel well enough, but you are not to go running around disturbing every- one else."

"Yes, Lady Araminta," I mur- mured.

Olivia was in the next bed. She smiled at me. "Do you want to play a game?" she asked. "Fairy G. came in when you were asleep yesterday and left us some cards."

"Great," I said and I hopped out of bed. "And no lessons for two days! Hurrah!"

Olivia shook her head. "Don't get too happy. Fairy G. said she and Queen Mother Matilda were going to check on us this evening to see if we were well enough to do our designs for the floral bouquets tomorrow."

I was shocked. "You mean, take the test here in Ruby Pillows?

While we're still sick?"

Lauren heard me and came to sit on the edge of my bed. "Isn't it awful? And we can't even pretend we're worse than we are, because Fairy G. always knows if you're sick or not."

I nodded. That's the trouble with Fairy Godmothers. They're just too smart. "Oh, well," I said. "We'd better enjoy ourselves while we can." And we settled down to a game of Snap.

By the time Fairy G. arrived that evening, I was back in bed. It's funny how one minute you can feel completely better, and the next, your legs get wobbly and it's actually rather nice to be lying back on soft, snow-white pillows.

Fairy G. swooped into the room and beamed at us, and Queen Mother Matilda sailed in after her.

"Now, my dears," Fairy G. boomed, "let's see how you're doing! Will you be well enough tomorrow to dazzle us all with your posies of roses? Or will you still be a bunch of faded flowers?"

"I'm sure they'll be quite all right," Queen Mother Matilda snapped. "A Perfect Princess must always continue with her duties, regardless of her personal circumstances." She didn't think Fairy G. was very funny.

Fairy G. didn't answer. She was feeling around in her enormous purse, and she finally pulled out the most beautiful pearl on a long silver chain.

"I knew it was in there somewhere!" she said cheerfully. "Does

anyone think they're too sick to take the test tomorrow?"

Gruella and Diamonde's hands shot up in the air.

"Hmm," Fairy G. said, and she eyed them thoughtfully. "Let's see. This is my latest magical invention—it's a Truth Teller!"

And she set the pearl swinging around and around.

"Oooh!" I gasped. "It's wonderful!"

"It is pretty, isn't it?" Fairy G. agreed. "Now, watch carefully. . . ."

"Funny kind of magic if you ask me," Diamonde whispered to Gruella. "It would be more useful if it made us better, but I suppose that would be much too much to ask for. Fairy G.'s only a *school* Fairy Godmother, after all."

I saw Fairy G. look at Diamonde. I was certain she'd heard what she had said, but she didn't scold her. Instead she smiled.

"I'm afraid I can't make you better, my dears, but the pearl will tell me if you really are too sick to take the test tomorrow."

We stared at the pearl, and as it went on circling around and around, it stopped shimmering and turned gray.

"Everyone's fine." Fairy G. gave

Diamonde and Gruella a brisk nod, and dropped the pearl back into her bag.

Gruella began to groan. "But I feel hot all over, and I've got a splitting headache."

"You'll be quite all right by tomorrow, Princess Gruella. Fairy G.'s magic is never wrong." Queen Mother Matilda wasn't at all sympathetic. "We'll see you in the morning." And she and Fairy G. hurried out of the room.

A moment later, Fairy G. popped her head back into our room. "Don't forget, my dears, there's a lovely prize for the winner,

and all her friends as well!" And she
smiled and disappeared.

We stared at one another after
Fairy G. had gone. "A lovely prize
for what?" Chloe asked.

"A prize for whoever makes the best bouquet, of course," Diamonde sneered. She gave me a cold look. "And we all know who thinks she's going to win!"

I shrugged and snuggled down in my bed. "We'll see what happens tomorrow," I said. "Good night!"

Chapter Three

I woke up early the following morning, and I felt amazing! I hopped out of bed, and after I'd collected a piece of paper and pencils from Lady Araminta's supply closet, I began drawing and coloring ideas for bouquets. I love flowers. My

27

parents have the biggest palace garden, and when I was little I used to spend a lot of time with the head gardener.

I hadn't been drawing for long when I had an idea. I decided I'd use lots of flowers, like pale blue love-in-a-mist, and the palest mauve and pink sweet peas, and white baby's breath—so the bouquet would look very delicate—and then I'd have trailing ivy mixed with the cutest pale pink and mauve ribbons.

I was really enjoying myself when I suddenly noticed that Gruella was looking over my shoulder.

"What's *that* stuff?" she asked.
"That fluffy stuff?"

I wanted to hide my picture, because I had a nasty feeling Gruella might copy my idea, but *A Perfect Princess always thinks the best of others.* I sighed and told her it

was love-in-a-mist.

"I'm going to make my bouquet with real flowers," Gruella said snootily. "Roses and lilies!" She pointed to my drawing of sweet peas. "Are those things supposed to be butterflies? That's silly. They'll fly away."

Before I could answer, Lady Araminta came sweeping into Ruby Pillows, clapping her hands to wake everyone up.

"No time for scribbling now, Princess Georgia," she told me as Gruella scurried off. I hastily folded my drawing and pushed it under my pillow.

"We've got a busy morning ahead of us," Lady Araminta went on, "and I want everything neat and tidy before Queen Mother Matilda arrives. And"—Lady Araminta looked very pleased— "we have the most delightful surprise! Your principal, Queen Fabiola, has decided to come to Ruby Pillows and judge your designs!"

She obviously expected us to be totally thrilled, so I began to clap. After a second or two, everyone else joined in, and Lady Araminta smiled approvingly.

"Quite right. Queen Fabiola has

already looked at all the drawings that the Rose Room, the Lavender Room, and the others did yesterday. Now it's your turn. Please make your beds and go to the Ruby Pillows dining hall for breakfast. Once you have finished, the dining

tables will be cleared and paper and markers will be set out for your test."

There was a lot of chatting about ideas over breakfast, but Diamonde and Gruella didn't join in. Instead, they kept whispering to each other. As soon as Queen Mother Matilda arrived, they rushed up to her and curtsied.

"Your Majesty," Diamonde said with her best smile, "please may we work together? We've had such a great idea!"

"That's right." Gruella curtsied again. "And we'd like to call it the Queen Mother Matilda Bouquet, in honor of you!"

Queen Mother Matilda looked thoughtful. "Well . . ." she began, "it is meant to be a bouquet for a Very Special Princess. . . ."

"*Please,*" Diamonde begged, and she smiled a horrible sickly smile.

"Very well, my dears." Queen Mother Matilda handed them a sheet of paper, and they hurried back to their table and started drawing.

"I'm truly delighted to see that at least two of you have prepared for this test," the Queen Mother said as she put the pile of drawing paper down. "The rest of you, begin as soon as you are ready—and don't forget to put your names on your designs!"

Two minutes later, the dining hall was very quiet as we began to sketch out our ideas.

After a while, Queen Mother Matilda began walking around and peering over our shoulders. I saw her nodding in a pleased kind of way as she looked at Gruella and Diamonde's drawing.

"Charming!" she said. "Really charming!"

She moved on to Olivia, and then to Jessica, and down the length of the table. By the time she reached me, I had nearly finished, and though I know it's wrong to boast, I was quite pleased with what I'd done. I waited for Queen Mother Matilda to nod at me, too, but she didn't. She stood very still, and gave me the coldest stare.

"Princess Georgia," she said, "this is not what I would expect from a Perfect Princess."

I stared at her in amazement. What did she mean?

Queen Mother Matilda made an angry *tsk-tsk* noise and frowned at me. "We'll have to see what Queen Fabiola has to say about this, Georgia. And if I'm not mistaken,

she's just arrived!"

The Queen Mother was right. A trumpeter leaped into the room and blew a loud *tantara-tara*! When he had finished, he bowed and

stood back to allow Queen Fabiola and Fairy G. to come marching past him.

Fairy G. was rubbing her ears. "Must he do that quite so loudly?" she grumbled.

Queen Fabiola waved her ear trumpet. "But it's such fun, Fairy G.! And I can hear it perfectly!" She beamed at all of us. "You think it's fun, don't you, my dears?"

We curtsied deeply and said, "Yes, Your Majesty," although our ears were ringing.

"Excellent! Excellent!" Our principal smiled at us. "And now let's see these lovely pictures of your

beautiful bouquets. The Rose
Room and the others did very well,
and I'd like to see what you've been
up to."

Queen Mother Matilda stepped forward, still holding my design. "One moment, Your Majesty," she said, and she sounded so serious. "We have a problem." And she handed Queen Fabiola my piece of paper.

Chapter Four

My heart started pounding in my chest as I watched Queen Fabiola turn my picture the right way up.

"But this is wonderful!" she said as she studied it.

Queen Mother Matilda shook her head. "Princess Gruella! Princess

Diamonde! Please bring your picture here," she ordered.

Gruella and Diamonde came skipping up. They curtsied and fluttered their eyelashes at Queen Fabiola, and Gruella murmured, "We're honored to show you our little idea, Your Majesty."

But Diamonde was peeping at the piece of paper in Queen Fabiola's hand.

"Oh!" she squealed and threw her arms in the air. "Gruella! Look! Look! Georgia's copied *our* design." And she gave me such a triumphant stare that I just knew they'd planned

exactly what they were going to do and say.

Queen Fabiola looked at the two pictures. They did look almost exactly the same.

"I'm afraid there's no doubt that Georgia is guilty," Queen Mother Matilda told our principal. "The twins began drawing long before anyone else."

"That's right," Gruella said smugly. "We did, didn't we, Diamonde? So that proves Georgia is a cheater!"

"Just one moment!" It was Fairy G. Her voice was sharp. "I think Princess Georgia should be allowed to say how she believes this strange coincidence has happened."

I looked at Fairy G. gratefully, but it was difficult to know what to say without being a horrible tattletale. I bobbed another little curtsey and said, "I'm afraid I can't explain. I did a sketch for my idea early on before breakfast, and then I drew it again for the competition."

"She's lying!" Diamonde interrupted. "She copied us! I know she did!"

"Silence!" When Fairy G. is angry she grows huge and looks really scary.

She towered above us all. Even Queen Fabiola looked taken aback.

"Can you show us this sketch?" Fairy G. asked me. Even though she was looking angry, she didn't sound too upset.

I was about to say I didn't know where it was—and then I remembered!

"Yes!" I said. "I pushed it under my pillow."

Queen Mother Matilda began to huff and to puff. "Surely there's no need for this, Fairy G.," she complained. "It seems to me it's a cut-and-dried case of cheating!"

Fairy G. opened her bag, pulled out her wonderful pearl, and set it swinging around and around. I gasped. It wasn't pearl-colored anymore—it was *black*!

"Someone is not telling the truth," she said and turned to Lady

Araminta. "Dear Lady, would you be so kind as to look under Georgia's pillow?"

Lady Araminta hurried off. My heart began to thump louder and louder. What if my picture wasn't there after all? But a moment later she was back with my crumpled drawing in her hand.

"Actually," she said, "I did see Princess Georgia busy drawing this morning. She was with Princess Gruella, just before breakfast."

Fairy G. nodded and hung the pearl over my drawing. At once it cleared and began to shimmer in the most beautiful way. Fairy G.

nodded again and held the pearl over Diamonde and Gruella's picture: First it turned a nasty green, and then slowly it darkened to black.

There was a long silence, and then Gruella began to whimper.

"We didn't *really* copy Georgia's picture. I must have just sort of noticed it when I was asking about the flowers. . . ."

"That's right," Diamonde agreed. "We must have copied it by mistake."

Queen Fabiola lifted up her ear trumpet. "What? What's that you're saying, child? A mistake? Who's made a mistake?"

"I think Princesses Gruella and Diamonde have made a mistake, Your Majesty," Fairy G. said. She sounded grim. "A very unpleasant mistake."

Diamonde looked at Gruella,

and Gruella looked at Diamonde.
They turned bright red, and then
Diamonde said, all in one breath,

"We're very, very sorry if it looked as if Georgia copied our picture because she didn't, and we didn't mean to make ours the same, but it just happened that way because we're so sick." And she grabbed Gruella's hand and they bolted out of the Ruby Pillows dining hall. Chloe was closest to the door, and she told me later that she saw them dive into their beds and pull their covers right up over their heads.

"I think," Fairy G. said calmly, "we'll leave the twins to think about what they've done."

Queen Mother Matilda looked flustered. "Do I understand it was the *twins* who were cheating?" she asked. She patted me on the head. "Oh, dear me! I'm so sorry, Georgia. I was much too hasty in my judgment!"

"I'm sure Princess Georgia will forgive you," Queen Fabiola said. "After all, there's no doubt in my mind that she's won the prize for the most beautiful bouquet. Fairy G., could I ask you to please wave your magic wand?"

Chapter Five

I didn't know where to look. Everything had happened so suddenly—instead of being in disgrace, I was the winner! I'd won the prize! And as Fairy G. waved her wand, flowers began to fall from the ceiling—and they were all the flowers I had chosen for my bouquet design!

"Come along, Poppy Room!" Fairy G. gave us a huge smile. "Georgia will tell you what to do! We want to see each of you make the most beautiful bouquet."

And we did. I do think Fairy G. must have added a little extra fairy dust, though, because the flowers almost flew into the right places, and the ribbons curled themselves into the prettiest loops and bows. In no time at all, we were each holding the most amazing bouquet—and I'm not being boastful. The flowers were so wonderful, and Fairy G.'s

magic had given them an extra
sparkle.

Queen Fabiola smiled at us.
"There!" she said. "Six beautiful
bouquets—for six Very Special

Princesses! And I think you'll find that they last for a long, long time. Isn't that right, Fairy G.?"

Fairy G. nodded. "They certainly will," she said. "Oh, and there's just one last thing I have to do." She took the pearl and began to twirl it around and around and around again. Gradually it began to shimmer and glow until it was as fabulous as it had been when we first saw it.

"Excellent!" Fairy G. said. "Although I think the poor thing is almost worn out. Let me try one last twirl."

And it was amazing!

Hanging up behind our chairs were the most adorable pearl-colored dresses you could ever imagine—and the sashes were pale pink, and blue, and mauve, to

match the flowers in our bouquets.

We looked at one another with wide eyes.

"Thank you!" we all said. "They're *wonderful*!"

"I told you there was a prize," Fairy G. said. "But that's quite enough excitement for now! You'll be back in Ruby Mansions tomorrow, so enjoy today, and no running around!"

"I'll make sure of that," Lady Araminta said firmly. "And now I think it's time for a little rest."

Queen Fabiola looked surprised. "Best?" she said. "Best? But we know who's best! It's the Poppy

Room! Didn't I just tell them?"

And we couldn't help laughing.

As Lady Araminta tucked us into our beds that night, I peeped at the bouquets on our bedside tables and I couldn't help thinking how lucky I was to be at Ruby Mansions. And I'm so lucky my friends are here, too—especially you.

What happens next?

FIND OUT IN

✦ Princess Olivia ✦
∽ AND THE ∽
✦ Velvet Cape ✦

Hello! I'm Princess Olivia, one of
the Poppy Room Princesses, and
I'm so pleased you're here too.
Maybe you know Chloe, Jessica,
Georgia, Lauren, and Amy?
They're my best friends, and
they're so nice! Not at all like the twins,
Diamonde and Gruella. I know Perfect
Princesses shouldn't say bad things about
other princesses, but those two are so
awful.

Visit all your favorite

The Tiara Club